I0765522

LENNAN & SMALLSY COMICS

VOLUME 1

LENNAN & SMALLSY COMICS

VOLUME I

SARA YAN

Illustrations by

Martin Richard

Illustrations by Martin Richard
Layout by Peggy Stockdale

ISBN 978-0-6457060-0-0 (paperback)
ISBN 978-0-6457060-1-7 (hardcover)
ISBN 978-0-6457060-2-4 (ebook)

www.lennanandsmallsy.com

To anyone who is hungry for change

CONTENTS

Introduction 9

Real Men 12
Flower Power 13
Thin Air 15
Greatest Gift 16
Push 17
Detention 18
Never Fall Down 20
Home Economics 21
Go Getter 22
Broccoli 23
Sweets Sell 24
Cool Dads 26
School Ordeal 27
Eat 29
Cooking Lesson 30
Emergency Dinner 31
Wacky Family 32
Like You 33
A Problem Like Milton 35
Feel the Fear 36
The Price of Friendship 37

Serve and Protect 38
Great Things 39
Bugs 40
Rude Mood 41
Milton's Grudge 42
Like Father Like Son 43
Threats 44
Parents 46
The View 48
Father's Insight 49
Permission 50
Big Bad Wolf 51
Rain Check 52
The Storm 54
Special Stuff 55
Big Hug 57
Earmuffs 58
The Problem 59
Car Nightmare 60
Don't Want To 62

Acknowledgements 65
Want More? 66

INTRODUCTION

How did I get here, you might ask?

Well, not long after escaping my own entrapment, I discovered that the readily available information on domestic violence was missing something. It seemed mostly centered on victim support services, with a huge lack of focus on the underlying causes.

One day, while cooking lunch, I found myself fuming over my potatoes. *"It's all 'helpline' this, and 'red flags' that,"* I thought to myself. *"Why isn't anyone talking about the causes? And why aren't people asking how and why we got here?"*

Suddenly I realised something.

Not only was there scant information on the causes of domestic violence, it was all but missing from the entertainment scene too. I found little to no films, television shows or literature that took on domestic violence as anything more than a plot device for cheap melodrama. And there were certainly no cartoons that addressed it.

I was determined to change this.

I created Lennan & Smallsy Comics to explore the causes and consequences of domestic violence.

The characters and storylines have been written specifically to break down the overwhelming landscape of family abuse into more graspable, bite-sized chunks.

For instance, my strips featuring Lennan and Justine show how fathers can impart their abusive tendencies onto their sons, who repeat the cycle of violence during courtship. And my strips containing Smallsy and Derek show that rejecting gender stereotypes and negative masculine ideals creates safe homes where women and children are nurtured and empowered.

Stories engage people in a uniquely compelling way. And cartoons have a clarity and simplicity that spark emotion and can cultivate powerful ideas. Cartoon characters have a way of seeping into the collective psyche and making ripples in society. They have an unrivalled propensity to become cultural icons that leave lasting impressions for generations to come.

I hope that Lennan and Smallsy will become one such icon by drawing awareness to the causes of domestic violence.

And in doing so, I hope that people will see that there's a real possibility for change.

REAL MEN
DO YOU THINK I'LL EVER BE A REAL MAN?

REAL MEN
THAT DEPENDS. HAVE YOU EVER PICKED ON SOMEONE SMALLER AND WEAKER THAN YOU?
NO

REAL MEN
SORRY, SMALLSY

REAL MEN
GUESS I'LL JUST SETTLE FOR BEING A GOOD PERSON

REAL MEN

FLOWER POWER

WHEN WE GET MARRIED, IT'LL BE THE BEST DAY OF MY LIFE!
MINE TOO!

WE'LL HAVE RED ROSES AND BLUE TABLECLOTHS!
I HATE BLUE

WE'LL HAVE A HORSE DRAWN CARRIAGE!
I WANT A LIMOUSINE

WE'LL HAVE HUNDREDS OF GUESTS, AND ALL MY FAMILY!
WHAT ABOUT MY FAMILY!
AND WHEN I SEE YOU, I'LL SAY, 'I DO!'

TO WHO? THIN AIR? I WON'T BE THERE!
LENNAN & SMALLSY COMICS

THIN AIR

GREATEST GIFT

AND FIVE!
WEEEEEEEE!

LET'S GO TO THE ROUNDABOUT!
HEY! WHAT ARE YOU DOING?

WHAT? FIVE PUSHES ON THE SWINGS MEANS I CAN HOLD YOUR HAND!
I SAY WHEN YOU CAN HOLD MY HAND

TEN PUSHES ON THE SWINGS MEANS I CAN GIVE YOU A HUG!
I SAY WHEN YOU CAN HUG ME

I CAN KISS YOU AFTER TWENTY PUSHES, BUT THAT'S ONLY ON THE ROUNDABOUT, AND WE HAVEN'T BEEN THERE YET
UGH!
LENNAN & SMALLSY COMICS

PUSH

DO YOU KNOW WHY YOU'RE IN DETENTION AGAIN, LENNAN?
BECAUSE I PUSHED JUSTINE ON THE PLAYGROUND
Ms Jemima
LENNAN & SMALLSY COMICS

WHY DID YOU PUSH JUSTINE ON THE PLAYGROUND?
BECAUSE SHE WOULDN'T LET ME PLAY WITH HER
LENNAN & SMALLSY COMICS

DO YOU ALWAYS HURT JUSTINE WHEN YOU GET ANGRY?
LENNAN & SMALLSY COMICS

ONLY IF SHE DOESN'T GIVE ME WHAT I WANT!
Ms Jemima
LENNAN & SMALLSY COMICS

DETENTION

NEVER FALL DOWN

HOME ECONOMICS

LENNAN, MY BOY! HOW'S YOUR DAD? STILL KEEPING OUR TOWN SAFE?
OUR TOWN, MAYBE
YOU TELL HIM HE'S WELCOME HERE ANYTIME!
LENNAN & SMALLSY COMICS

AND WHAT ABOUT YOU, MY LAD? HOW'S YOUR MOTHER?
SHE GOT PROMOTED!
LENNAN & SMALLSY COMICS

A GO GETTER, 'EH? THAT'S ADORABLE! ENJOY YOUR ICE CREAM, MY BOY!
Campbell's
LENNAN & SMALLSY COMICS

I THOUGHT YOU LIKED THAT FLAVOUR!
IT HAS A YUCKY AFTERTASTE
LENNAN & SMALLSY COMICS

GO GETTER

MR CAMPBELL, HOW CAN I MAKE JUSTINE DO WHAT I WANT?
MY DEAR BOY, LET ME ANSWER YOU THIS WAY. WHY DO YOU COME TO MY STORE?
BECAUSE YOU MAKE THE BEST ICE CREAM IN TOWN!
LENNAN & SMALLSY COMICS

WHAT IF I DIDN'T SELL ICE CREAM? WHAT IF I SOLD... BROCCOLI INSTEAD?
I HATE BROCCOLI! I WANT ICE CREAM!
WHY?
LENNAN & SMALLSY COMICS

BECAUSE IT'S SWEET!
EXACTLY!
I DON'T GET IT...
LENNAN & SMALLSY COMICS

THE BOY WHO'S SWEET GETS THE TREAT, LENNAN. DON'T FORGET IT
LENNAN & SMALLSY COMICS

BROCCOLI

I CAN'T WAIT TO WORK FOR YOU, MR CAMPBELL!
WHEN DO I START?
IT'S A PLEASURE HAVING SUCH A PRETTY GIRL IN MY SHOP
LENNAN & SMALLSY COMICS

AS SOON AS YOU PUT THESE ON!
LENNAN & SMALLSY COMICS

WILL I LEARN THE SECRET RECIPE OF YOUR ICE CREAMS? OR HELP PLAN YOUR BUSINESS STRATEGY?
MY DEAR GIRL, YOU'LL HAVE THE MOST IMPORTANT JOB OF ALL! FOLLOW ME!
LENNAN & SMALLSY COMICS

YOU'LL GREET PASSERSBY! WHEN THEY SEE HOW LOVELY YOU ARE, MY SWEETS WILL SELL THEMSELVES
Campbell's
Sweets & Treats
LENNAN & SMALLSY COMICS

SWEETS SELL

YUM! MY DAD MADE ROAST BEEF ON RYE!
YOUR DAD MADE YOU LUNCH? MY DAD NEVER COOKS

MY DAD'S A GOOD COOK
MY DAD SAYS THE KITCHEN IS A MOTHER'S DOMAIN

WHAT'S IT TASTE LIKE?

TASTES LIKE LUNCH FROM A COOL DAD DOMAIN

COOL DADS

SCHOOL ORDEAL

GR8 FMLY

THIS LOOKS DELICIOUS, MRS ROBERTS!
LENNAN & SMALLSY COMICS

OH, I CAN'T TAKE CREDIT. DEREK MADE IT!
THANKS, DAD!
LENNAN & SMALLSY COMICS

IF HE COOKS, THEN WHAT DO YOU DO?
LENNAN & SMALLSY COMICS

EAT!
HA!
HA!
HA!
LENNAN & SMALLSY COMICS

EAT

COOKING LESSON

EMERGENCY DINNER

WACKY FAMILY

HEY LIONEL!
IT'S DEREK. TRY THIS!
YEAH, HI DAMON

IT'S GOOD
LENNAN MADE IT

BUT I NEVER TAUGHT HIM TO COOK
I DID! I SHOWED HIM HOW TO MAKE THEM! HOW COOL IS THAT? SOON HE'LL BE A PRO, LIKE ME!

LIKE YOU, 'EH

LIKE YOU

A PROBLEM LIKE MILTON

FEEL THE FEAR

THE PRICE OF FRIENDSHIP

SERVE AND PROTECT

GREAT THINGS

WHAT ARE YOU RAISING MONEY FOR?
"ALL PROFITS GO TO SHELTERS FOR VICTIMS FLEEING FAMILY CRISES"
I HAD THAT

A FAMILY CRISIS?
YEP. WE HAD TO MOVE OUT FOR A WEEK WHILE THEY SPRAYED OUR HOUSE
ME TOO! WE HAD SO MANY BUGS, THEY NEARLY CARRIED ME OUT OF THE HOUSE!

I DON'T THINK THE CRISIS IS BUGS
A MIDLIFE CRISIS THEN?
NO...

SMALLSY, WHAT ELSE IS SO BAD THAT TOBIAS' MUM MAKES HIM SELL BISCUITS IN SCHOOL HOLIDAYS? BUGS ARE OUR TOWN'S BIGGEST PROBLEM!

IF YOU KEEP SPILLING CRUMBS, THEY WILL BE
LENNAN & SMALLSY COMICS

BUGS

GIMME TWO MORE OF THE NUT ONES
SURE THING, MR RICHARDS!
WE ALSO HAVE CHOCOLATE CHIP, CHOCOLATE CREAM, AND MY PERSONAL FAVOURITE, TRIPLE RIPPLE CHOCOLATE
LENNAN & SMALLSY COMICS

YOUR MONEY WILL HELP BUILD SAFE HAVENS FOR WOMEN IN THE COMMUNITY!
HOLIDAY HOMES? FOR WOMEN? COOL!
LENNAN & SMALLSY COMICS

THESE COOKIES TASTE LIKE CRAP
LENNAN & SMALLSY COMICS

SLAM!!
WHY THE RUDE MOOD CHANGE?
I TOLD YOU WE SHOULD ONLY SELL THE CHOCOLATE ONES!
LENNAN & SMALLSY COMICS

RUDE MOOD

MILTON'S GRUDGE

LIKE FATHER LIKE SON

HEY LENNAN, I'VE GOT A FEELING YOUR FRIENDSHIP WITH SMALLSY IS GONNA BE, UM, CUT SHORT, HE HE
YEAH SURE, MILTON

IF YOU LIKE ART, THEN YOU'RE GONNA LOVE MY MASTERPIECE
ALRIGHT, THAT'S IT, I'M TELLING MS JEMIMA! I AM GETTING SO SICK OF YOU AND ALL YOUR EMPTY-

THREATS

THREATS

I HATE MY PARENTS
LENNAN & SMALLSY COMICS

HOW CAN YOU SAY THAT? THEY'RE YOUR PARENTS!
ALL THEY DO IS ARGUE. IT NEVER ENDS
LENNAN & SMALLSY COMICS

WHEN MY PARENTS ARGUE, THEY HOLD A FAMILY MEETING. THEY EACH TAKE TURNS TALKING AND LISTENING. I ALWAYS KNOW WHEN THEY'VE RESOLVED IT, 'CAUSE THEY HUG EACH OTHER AFTER. SOMETIMES THEY HUG ME TOO. WHAT DO YOU DO WHEN YOUR PARENTS ARGUE?
LENNAN & SMALLSY COMICS

I GET IN MY WARDROBE AND SHUT THE DOOR
LENNAN & SMALLSY COMICS

PARENTS

I LOVE IT UP HERE!
THE VIEW IS AMAZING!

I DON'T CARE ABOUT THE VIEW
THEN WHY DO YOU COME HERE?

WHEN I'M UP HERE, NOTHING CAN GET ME!
LIKE WHAT?

MY DAD

THE VIEW

FATHER'S INSIGHT

LENNAN, I NEED YOUR PERMISSION SLIP. YOU CAN'T GO ON THE FIELD TRIP WITHOUT IT
I KNOW
LENNAN & SMALLSY COMICS

HAS YOUR MUM SIGNED IT YET?
NO, SHE'S WAITING
WAITING FOR WHAT?
LENNAN & SMALLSY COMICS

FOR MY DAD TO GIVE HER PERMISSION TO SIGN IT!
LENNAN & SMALLSY COMICS

LENNAN & SMALLSY COMICS

PERMISSION

LENNAN, LET ME TALK TO YOUR MUM. I CAN HELP HER SIGN YOUR PERMISSION SLIP
HOW? YOU'RE NOT MY DAD
NO, BUT PERHAPS I CAN HELP WITH SOME OTHER PROBLEMS
Ms Jemima

WHAT OTHER PROBLEMS?
OH, UM, NOTHING MUCH. JUST SOME FAMILY STUFF
Ms Jemima

IT'S ME, ISN'T IT! I'M THE PROBLEM! I KNEW IT! LET'S ALL BLAME LENNAN, THE BIG BAD WOLF!
NO, OF COURSE NOT! I JUST WANT TO HELP YOUR MUM WITH WHATEVER'S GOING ON SO THAT YOU CAN GO ON THE FIELD TRIP!

SO IT'S NOT ABOUT ME?
NO. I PROMISE
Ms Jemima

AND THERE'S NO BIG BAD WOLF?
WELL, ACTUALLY...
LENNAN & SMALLSY COMICS

BIG BAD WOLF

RICHARDS' RESIDENCE?
MRS RICHARDS, IT'S MS JEMIMA. I WAS HOPING TO SEE YOU ABOUT THE SCHOOL FIELD TRIP. IT'S NEXT WEEK, BUT WE DON'T HAVE LENNAN'S PERMISSION SLIP. HOW'S THIS AFTERNOON FOR YOU?
LENNAN & SMALLSY COMICS

OH, I'M SORRY ABOUT THAT! OF COURSE I'LL SEE YOU. THIS AFTERNOON'S FINE, BUT I DON'T THINK LIONEL CAN COME
THAT'S OK! I WAS ACTUALLY HOPING TO SPEAK WITH YOU ALONE
Ms Jemima

REALLY? THAT WOULD BE NICE. THANK YOU, MS JEMIMA. I'M LOOKING FORWARD TO IT
ME TOO! SEE YOU SOON! DRIVE SAFE IN THIS WEATHER!
Ms Jem

UM, SPEAKING OF WEATHER, I'LL HAVE TO TAKE A RAIN CHECK
Ms Je
LENNAN & SMALLSY COMICS

RAIN CHECK

DAD, CAN I ASK YOU SOMETHING?
SURE!
ARE ALL FAMILIES LIKE OURS?

WHAT MADE YOU ASK THAT, SON?
WELL, WHENEVER I'M AT LENNAN'S HOUSE, THINGS FEEL... DIFFERENT

SON, LISTEN. FAMILIES ARE JUST LIKE PLANTS! YOU HAVE TO WATER THEM WITH LOVE AND PROTECT THEM FROM STORMS!
THE DIFFERENCES DON'T MATTER, AS LONG AS EVERYONE IN THE HOUSE IS SAFE AND HAPPY! SEE?
I THINK SO. THANKS, DAD!

ANYTIME, SON! SWEET DREAMS!
GOOD NIGHT, DAD

BUT WHAT IF THE STORM'S INSIDE THE HOUSE?
LENNAN & SMALLSY COMICS

THE STORM

SPECIAL STUFF

HEY SWEETIE. WHERE'S LENNAN? ISN'T HE SLEEPING OVER?
LENNAN CAN'T COME. HE SAYS HE SHOULD STAY WITH HIS MUM TONIGHT. SOMETHING ABOUT HIS DAD BEING MADDER THAN USUAL

OH, DEAR. I WISH WE COULD DO SOMETHING TO HELP
THAT'S IT! MRS RICHARDS CAN STAY HERE TOO! SHE CAN HAVE MY BED, AND I'LL CAMP WITH YOU AND DAD!

I DON'T KNOW, SWEETIE. YOUR BED'S A BIT SMALL
I'LL BUY A NEW ONE! I'VE GOT NEARLY TWENTY DOLLARS SAVED UP! I'LL BUY THE BIGGEST BED IN THE STORE!

TELL YOU WHAT. INSTEAD OF A BIG BED, WHY DON'T WE GIVE LENNAN'S MUM SOMETHING ELSE?
WHAT?
COME HERE

A BIG HUG
LENNAN & SMALLSY COMICS

BIG HUG

HE JUST YELLS AND YELLS. DAY AND NIGHT
YOUR DAD? THAT SOUNDS SCARY
LENNAN, YOUR DAD REMINDS ME OF THE DOG ON OUR BLOCK. IT BARKS AND BARKS. DAY AND NIGHT. DROVE US CRAZY!
LENNAN & SMALLSY COMICS

DID YOU TALK TO THE OWNER?
NO WAY! NO ONE CAN GO NEAR THE PLACE, OR THE DOG WILL ATTACK!
LENNAN & SMALLSY COMICS

SO THAT'S IT? YOU JUST GAVE UP?
OH, NO! WE DIDN'T LET THAT DOG RUIN OUR LIVES. WE FOUND SOMETHING THAT FIXED THE PROBLEM FOR GOOD!
WHAT?
LENNAN & SMALLSY COMICS

EARMUFFS
CAN I BORROW THE EARMUFFS? TOBIAS?
HE CAN'T HEAR YOU, LENNAN
LENNAN & SMALLSY COMICS

EARMUFFS

MR AND MRS RICHARDS, LENNAN'S MARKS ARE DOWN. THEY'RE EVEN WORSE THAN LAST YEAR. IS EVERYTHING OK AT HOME?
NOW THAT YOU MENTION IT –
LENNAN & SMALLSY COMICS

LISTEN, JEMIMA, I WORK HARD TO PROVIDE FOR MY SON, SO I DON'T NEED THESE ACCUSATIONS
IT'S 'MS' JEMIMA. AND I WAS MORE REFERRING TO THE EMOTIONAL CLIMATE AT HOME. WHAT WERE YOU SAYING, MRS RICHARDS?
WELL –
Ms Jemima
LENNAN & SMALLSY COMICS

IF HIS MARKS ARE LOW, THAT'S ON YOU. YOU'RE THE TEACHER. YOU SHOULD BE ABLE TO SEE THE PROBLEM
LENNAN & SMALLSY COMICS

OH, I SEE THE PROBLEM
LENNAN & SMALLSY COMICS

THE PROBLEM

CAR NIGHTMARE

SMALLSY, I'M NOT LIKE MY DAD, RIGHT?
WELL... HONESTLY?
LENNAN & SMALLSY COMICS

I KNEW IT! I'M TURNING INTO HIM!
HOLD ON
FORGET IT, SMALLSY, THERE'S NO HOPE! DON'T YOU SEE? I'M DOOMED!
LENNAN & SMALLSY COMICS

YOU'RE NOT DOOMED. AND THERE IS HOPE. YOU'RE NOT GONNA TURN OUT LIKE YOUR DAD
I'M NOT?
NO
LENNAN & SMALLSY COMICS

NOT IF YOU DON'T WANT TO
LENNAN & SMALLSY COMICS

DON'T WANT TO

Let's end
domestic violence

ACKNOWLEDGEMENTS

I'm grateful to my family for their support, and for understanding why I created Lennan & Smallsy Comics in the first place. Seeing them get excited as the series unfolds has been wonderful. Keep watching, everyone, 'cause I'm only just getting started!

I also want to say a big thank you to Martin for his incredible talent and ongoing effort in bringing my series onto the page so beautifully, and for seeming to grasp the emotional heart of my stories with so much insight. You are a national treasure!

And finally, I want to thank 'Derek.'

For everything.

WANT MORE?

Visit my website for regular updates, blog posts and behind the scenes news on Lennan & Smallsy Comics.

Join the conversation on domestic violence.
Subscribe to my newsletter.

LENNANANDSMALLSY.COM

SCAN ME

Follow Lennan & Smallsy Comics on social media.